2021

For Liz, with all my love
M. J. D.

With thanks to Walker Books
J. A.

Text copyright © 1999 Malachy Doyle
Illustrations copyright © 1999 Judith Allibone

First U.S. edition 1999

Library of Congress Cataloging-in-Publication Data

Doyle, Malachy.
Jody's beans / Malachy Doyle : illustrated by Judith Allibone. —
1st U.S. ed.
p. cm.
Summary: From spring to fall with the help of her grandfather,
Jody learns to plant, care for, harvest, prepare, and eat some runner beans.
ISBN 0–7636–0687–1
[1. Scarlet runner beans—Fiction.   2. Beans—Fiction.
3. Grandfather—Fiction.]
I. Allibone, Judith, ill.   II. Title.
PZ7.D775Jo   1999
[E]—dc21   98–40634

4 6 8 10 9 7 5 3

Printed in Hong Kong

This book was typeset in Usherwood.
The pictures were done in ink and watercolor.

Candlewick Press
2067 Massachusetts Avenue
Cambridge, Massachusetts 02140

JODY'S BEANS

Malachy Doyle

illustrated by Judith Allibone

CANDLEWICK PRESS
CAMBRIDGE, MASSACHUSETTS

It was springtime, and Jody's Granda
came to visit.

He brought Jody a packet of runner beans.

They counted them out on
the kitchen table.

". . . nine, ten, eleven, twelve," said Granda.

"That's enough."

They went out into the garden and found
the sunniest spot where the wind never blew.

They dug the soil and pulled out
all the weeds, mixed in some compost,
and raked it over.

Then Jody made twelve holes in a circle,
and put one seed in each.

"Don't forget to
water them, Jody,"
said Granda.

"What do runner beans look like,
Granda?" asked Jody.

"Wait and see,"
said Granda.
"Wait and see."

Soon the tiny green plants pushed their way
up through the dark brown soil.

Jody watered them
every day, unless it rained,
just as she'd been told.

One day the phone rang. It was Granda.

"Hello, Jody," he said.
"How are the beans?"

"They're growing
fast," said Jody.

"Good," said Granda. "Now listen closely.
This is what I want you to do . . ."

Jody went down to her vegetable patch
and pulled out the smallest plants.
Now the strongest ones
had plenty of room to grow.

Soon they were as

tall as the cat.

When Granda came to visit again,

he pushed six long canes in the ground beside

the plants, and tied them together at the top.

He looped string around and around

the poles all the way up

from the bottom.

"It's like
a teepee,"
said Jody.

The next few weeks were hot.

The sun burned down on the garden.

Jody watered her plants every day.

They snaked up the teepee,

hooking themselves onto the string

as they went.

16

"Granda," she said on the phone,
"they're bigger than me now!"

"That's great, Jody,"
said Granda.

"How big will
they get?"
Jody asked.

"Wait and see," said Granda.
"Wait and see."

Then the rain came.

Lots and lots of it.

Jody hardly had to water the plants at all.

They grew bigger every day,
and bright red flowers
burst out all over them.

"They're so beautiful,
Dad," said Jody.

After the warm
sunny days returned,
the first beans
appeared.

The plants reached the
tops of the poles, and Granda
came to visit again.

"They're even taller
than you, Granda!"
said Jody.

"They're wonderful beans, Jody,"
Granda said, pinching the tips at the
tops of the poles. "You must have a green
thumb, just like your Granda."

"Will the baby have a green thumb
too, Granda?" asked Jody.

"Wait and see,"
said Granda.
"Wait and see."

   21

"It's time to find out what they taste like," said Granda.

"Oh," said Jody, "I didn't know we were going to eat them."

So Jody and Granda picked handfuls of long thin green beans.

They topped
and tailed them,

sliced and boiled them,

and served them with butter.

"Mmm!" said Mom. "They're delicious."

The beans grew and grew,
right into the fall.

Jody picked them every day.

If she missed one, it grew hard and knobby.

Mom had to cut the stringy edges off.

It didn't taste as nice.

At the end of the fall Granda and Jody
picked the very last beans.

They were the ones right up
at the top of the poles
where Jody couldn't reach.

They were gigantic!

"They're no good,"
said Jody sadly.

"Oh, yes they are,"
said Granda.

And he opened them up,
took out the seeds, and spread
the twelve biggest
ones in a circle on
the kitchen table.

"Do you know what these are for, Jody?"
he asked.

"Yes, Granda," said Jody, smiling.
"They're next year's runner beans!"

"And how tall do you think they'll grow?"
asked Granda.

"Wait and see,
Granda,"
said Jody.
"Wait and see."

Index

Look up the pages to find out
about all these bean things.